It's Perfectly True!

It's Perfectly True!

adapted from
Hans Christian Andersen

and illustrated by
Janet Stevens

Holiday House / New York

Thank you, *Timmie Poh*, for the idea and thank you, *Virginia Westerberg*, for some Danish inspiration

Library of Congress Cataloging-in-Publication Data

Stevens, Janet.
   It's perfectly true.

   Summary: By the time a chicken's innocent remark
about losing a feather is passed on from one bird to
another, it turns into a wild story about the suicidal
deaths of five lovesick hens.
   [1. Chickens—Fiction.   2. Birds—Fiction.
3. Humorous stories]   I. Title.   II. Title: It is
perfectly true.
PZ7.S84452It   1988   [E]   87–7567
ISBN 0–8234–0672–5

"It's a monstrous story!" said a hen. "It's a horrible story, and it took place in a henhouse at the other end of town. When I think about what happened, it scares me so much, I can't close my eyes! I'm afraid to sleep on my perch!"

And then she told the story. It was so scary, the feathers of the other hens stood up and the rooster's comb fell down. It's perfectly true!

Now, let's go back to the beginning, where the story started in a henhouse at the other end of town . . .

The sun had gone down, and the hens had flown up to their roost. Among them was a hen with white feathers and stumpy legs. She was respectable and laid her eggs every day. As she settled into her perch, she pecked at her feathers, and one little feather fell out.

"There it goes," she said. "The more I peck out my feathers, the more beautiful I become."

This was said in fun, for she was a jolly hen as well as being respectable. Then she fell asleep.

It was dark, and the chickens nestled side by side. The hen that sat nearest to the one that had lost a feather was still awake. She had heard the jolly hen talking to herself. The wise thing would have been to keep quiet if she wanted to live in peace with her neighbors. But she could not help telling the hen next to her, "Did you hear what was said? I won't mention any names, but there's a hen here who says she's going to peck out her feathers to look more beautiful. If I were a rooster, I would despise her!"

An owl family with sharp ears lived above the henhouse. The owls heard every word of the hen's story. The mother owl rolled her eyes and flapped her wings.

"Don't listen," she said to her children, "but I'm sure you've heard it anyway. I heard it with my own ears, and one has to hear a lot before one's ears fall off. What's the world coming to if a hen is so improper as to peck out all her feathers in front of a rooster!"

"Hush!" said the father owl. "That story's not fit for our children to hear!"

"I must tell our neighbor about it," said the mother owl. "She is such a proper owl." And she flew away.

"Have you heard the news?" hooted the mother owl. "There is a hen who has pecked out all her feathers to impress a rooster. She must be freezing to death, if she isn't dead already. Hoot! Hoot!"

The mother owl hooted so loudly that the pigeons below could not help overhearing.

"Where? Where?" they cooed.

"Next door. I have *almost* seen it with my own eyes," said the mother owl. "It's a shocking story, but it's perfectly true!"

"It's true! It's true! Every word," cooed the pigeons, spreading the news. "There's a hen, maybe two, and they have pecked out all their feathers in order to look different from the other hens and get the rooster to notice them. They have played a dangerous game, for without feathers, they could die from the cold. And they have dropped dead, both of them!"

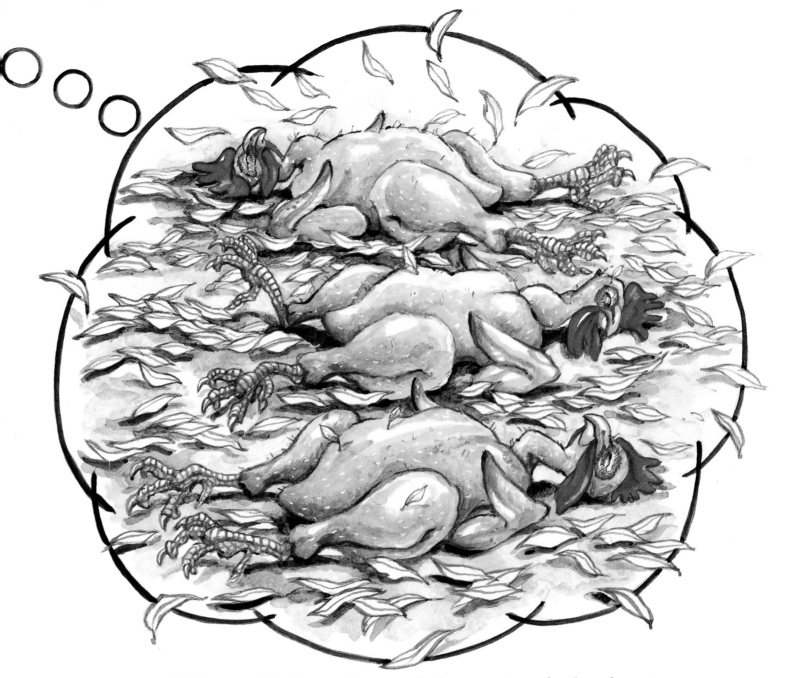

"Wake up! Wake up!" crowed the rooster who lived next to the pigeons. He flew up to the fence, his eyes heavy with sleep. "Three hens have died of a broken heart. It's a dreadful story! I can't keep it to myself. Pass it on!"

"Pass it on! Pass it on!" the bats screeched. "Pass it on!
Pass it on!" the hens clucked and the roosters crowed.

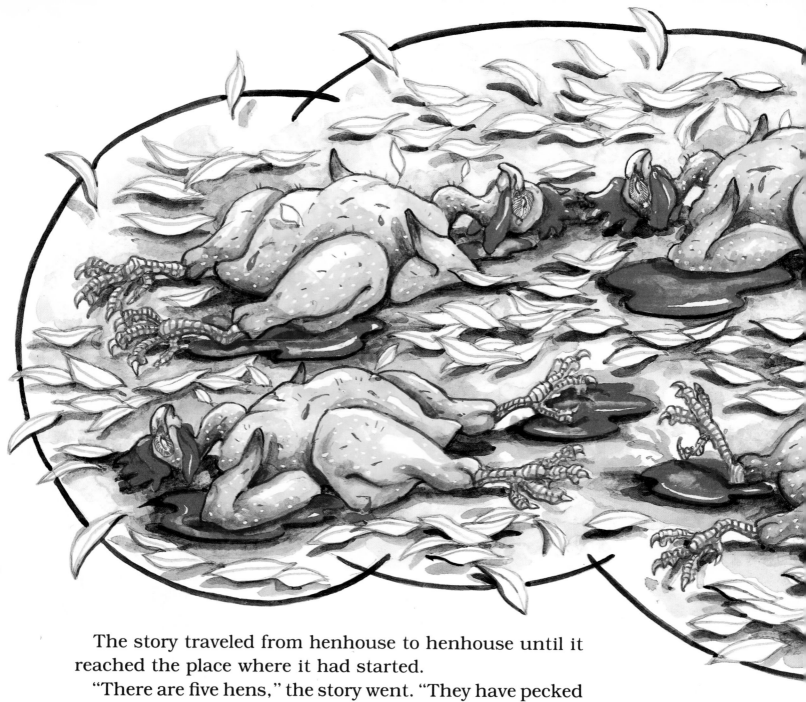

The story traveled from henhouse to henhouse until it reached the place where it had started.

"There are five hens," the story went. "They have pecked out all their feathers and have grown skinny and unhappy for the love of a rooster. Then they pecked each other until they bled to death, a disgrace to their families and a loss to their owner."

The hen who lost the one little feather naturally did not recognize the story. Since she was a decent and respectable hen, she said, "I despise such hens. But there are others like that. Such a horrible story should not be kept secret. I will see that it gets printed in the newspaper, so that the whole country will know. It will serve those hens right, and their families, too!"

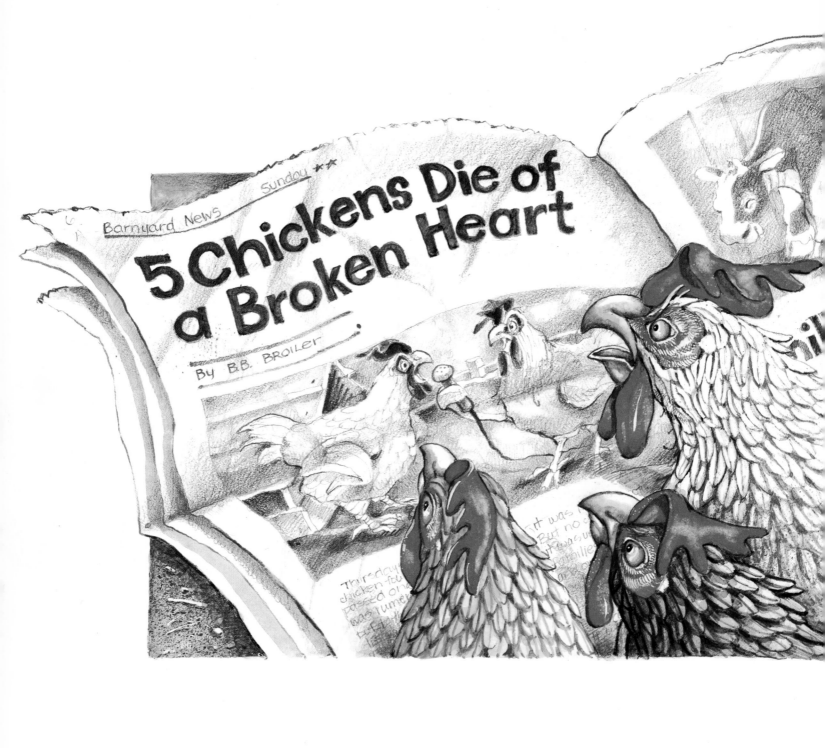

And it *was* printed in the newspaper, and it's perfectly
true . . . one little feather can become five dead hens!